BEAR ON THE LOOSE!

BY HILDE LYSIAK
WITH MATTHEW LYSIAK

ILLUSTRATED BY
JOANNE LEW-VRIETHOFF

BRANCHES
SCHOLASTIC INC.

To my Mammy, Martha Thrash

Copyright © 2017 by Hilde Lysiak and Matthew Lysiak
Illustrations copyright © 2017 by Joanne Lew-Vriethoff

Jacket photos © Dreamstime: Kavee Pathomboon, Frbird; _human/Thinkstock.

Photos ©: cover spirals and throughout: Kavee Pathomboon/Dreamstime; back cover paper: Frbird/
Dreamstime; back cover tape: _human/Thinkstock; back cover paper clip: Picsfive/Dreamstime; 88
paper clips and throughout: Fosin2/Thinkstock; 88 pins: Picsfive/Dreamstime; 88 bottom: Courtesy
of Joanne Lew-Vriethoff; 88 background: Leo Lintang/Dreamstime.

Library of Congress Cataloging-in-Publication Data

Names: Lysiak, Hilde, author. | Lysiak, Matthew, author. | Lew-Vriethoff, Joanne, illustrator.
Title: Bear on the Loose! / by Hilde Lysiak, with Matthew Lysiak ; illustrated by Joanne Lew-Vriethoff.
Description: First edition. | New York, NY : Branches/Scholastic Inc., 2017. |
Series: Hilde Cracks the Case | Summary: When she hears reports of a bear roaming
the backyards of Selinsgrove, Hilde and her sister/photographer Izzy are determined
to get the story for their own newspaper, the Orange Street News—but when they
find out the culprit is a black bear cub, their scoop turns into a rescue mission.
Identifiers: LCCN 2016059061| ISBN 9781338141580 (paperback) | ISBN 9781338141597 (hardcover)
Subjects: LCSH: Lysiak, Hilde—Juvenile fiction. | Reporters and reporting—Juvenile fiction. | Black
bear—Juvenile fiction | Wildlife rescue—Juvenile fiction | Sisters—Juvenile fiction | Detective and
mystery stories | CYAC: Mystery and detective stories | Reporters and reporting—Fiction | Black
bear—Fiction | Bears—Fiction | Wildlife rescue—Fiction | Sisters—Fiction | GSAFD: Mystery fiction |
LCGFT: Detective and mystery fiction

Classification: LCC PZ7.1.L97 Be 2017 | DDC 813.6 [Fic]—dc23
LC record available at https://lccn.loc.gov/2016059061

10 9 8 7 6 5 4 3 2   19 20 21

Printed in China 62
First edition, November 2017
Edited by Katie Carella
Book design by Baily Crawford

Table of Contents

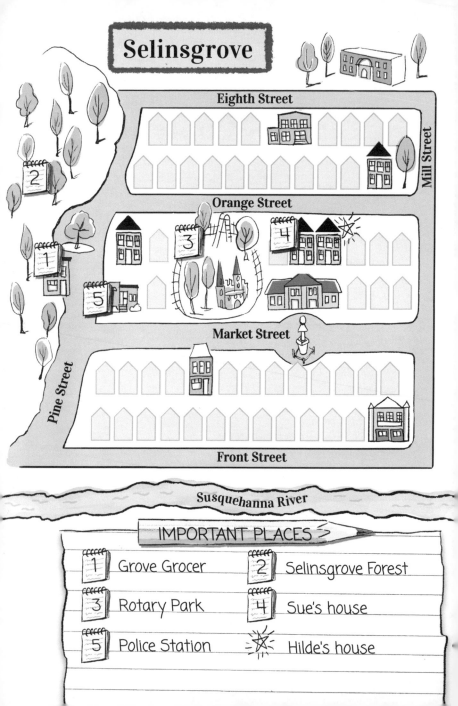

Introduction

Hi! My name is Hilde. (It rhymes with *build-y!*) I may be only nine years old, but I'm a serious reporter.

I learned all about newspapers from my dad. He used to be a reporter in New York City! I loved going with him to the scene of the crime. Each story was a puzzle. To put the pieces together, we had to answer six questions: Who? What? When? Where? Why? How? Then we'd solve the mystery!

I knew right away I wanted to be a reporter. But I also knew that no big newspaper was going to hire a kid. Did I let that stop me? Not a chance! That's why I created a paper for my hometown: the *Orange Street News.*

Now all I needed were stories that would make people want to read my paper. I wasn't going to find those sitting at home! Being a reporter means going out and hunting down the news. And there's no telling where a story will take me . . .

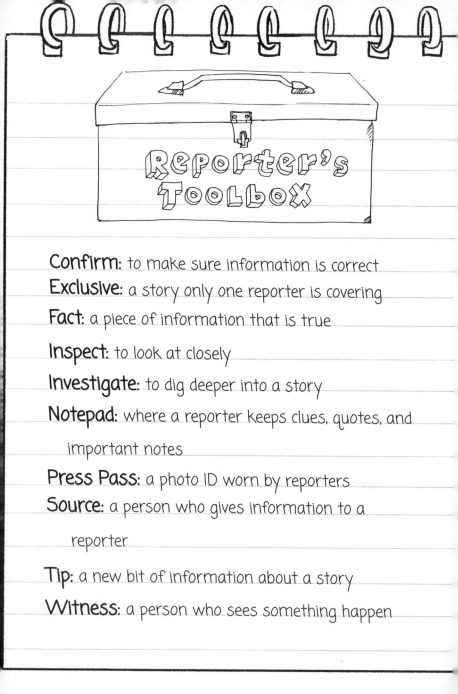

Reporter's Toolbox

Confirm: to make sure information is correct

Exclusive: a story only one reporter is covering

Fact: a piece of information that is true

Inspect: to look at closely

Investigate: to dig deeper into a story

Notepad: where a reporter keeps clues, quotes, and important notes

Press Pass: a photo ID worn by reporters

Source: a person who gives information to a reporter

Tip: a new bit of information about a story

Witness: a person who sees something happen

1 Police Chase

Officer Dee looked like a blur of blue as he sprinted down Market Street.

My older sister, Izzy, pedaled while I stood on her bike pegs. We raced to catch up to the police officer. Officer Dee is my most reliable source at the Selinsgrove Police Department.

"Do you really think there's a bear in town?" Izzy asked.

It may sound crazy, but Izzy and I had both heard the same thing: a call on Officer Dee's police radio saying there was a bear on the loose in Selinsgrove.

"Every tip needs to be confirmed!" I called up to her. "That means finding the facts. Pedal faster, Izzy!"

My heart was racing. People love animal stories — and a good story with a picture of a bear in it could be our biggest story yet!

Izzy pumped her legs harder. "I'm pedaling as fast as I can!" she said.

Officer Dee took a right on Pine. I clung to Izzy's shoulders as she made a sharp turn.

I had a good tip about *what* happened: *a bear was on the loose.* But I needed a lot more answers if I wanted to have a story fit for the *Orange Street News.*

Who? What? When? Where? Why? How?

Officer Dee was fast.
But Izzy on a bike was faster.

We were catching up when he ran onto the grass beside Grove Grocer.

Grove Grocer is the most popular store in town. Their famous beef jerky is one of my all-time favorite snacks.

"Officer Dee just ran behind the store!" Izzy said.

I hopped off Izzy's bike.

"Come on! Let's investigate," I said.

We ran behind Grove Grocer — and couldn't believe what we saw next!

2 The First Clue

Banana peels, coffee grounds, cardboard boxes, and all kinds of trash dotted the green grass behind Grove Grocer. It looked like a tornado had struck a garbage truck full of, well, garbage! The mess stretched all the way back to Selinsgrove Forest.

"Gross!" Izzy said. She began taking pictures.

I spotted Officer Dee right away. He was already busy talking to Mr. Troutman, the owner of Grove Grocer. The two of them were pointing to a red bird feeder lying on the ground.

Why are they staring at a bird feeder?

A reporter knows to never interrupt a police officer during an interview. But I still had to investigate. I pulled out my notepad and stood off to the side, listening.

I tried to get a good look at the feeder. And when I did, my eyes almost bulged out of my head!

The black metal pole that held up the feeder looked like it had been pulled out of the ground. Instead of a straight line, it was twisted into the shape of an *L*.

I got Izzy's attention and pointed at the feeder. She ran over and said, "It looks like that thing was tossed by an angry dinosaur!"

We knelt down for a closer look . . .

There were five large scratch marks on the feeder!

I jotted some notes.

Finally, Officer Dee walked away from Mr. Troutman. He nodded at me before he began inspecting the scene. That was his way of letting me know he was finished with the witness.

I saw my opening.

"Hi, Mr. Troutman,"
I said, walking over.

"Hi, Hilde," he said. "If you are looking for beef jerky you'll have to come back tomorrow. I closed up early — so I can clean up this mess."

"I'm actually here on business," I said, pointing to my press pass. "I'm reporting for my newspaper, the *Orange Street News*. I wanted to ask you some questions about what happened today."

"Sure. Well, I was inside getting ready to close the store when I heard loud clanging noises," he said.

"Clanging noises?" I asked.

"Yeah, it sounded like someone was banging on my garbage cans like they were drums," he added.

9

"What happened next?" I asked.

"I walked around back, expecting to yell at some rowdy teenagers," Mr. Troutman continued. "But that's when I saw it!"

3 Mangled and Clawed!

"What did you see, Mr. Troutman?" I asked. I held my pen to my notepad.

"That's when I saw my mangled bird feeder," said Mr. Troutman. "And when I took a closer look, I found *this* stuck to the feeder!"

He held up a small tuft of black fur.

"What is it?" I asked.

"I'm no animal expert, but I believe it's fur from a large bear!" he said.

A clue!

WHO: a bear, but what type of bear?

WHERE: behind the Grove Grocer

WHAT: trash cans tipped over and twisted bird pole and scratched feeder

Izzy took a picture of Mr. Troutman with the feeder. A great newspaper picture is one that can help tell the story. I knew this was going to be an amazing shot!

Click!

Then she snapped a close-up of the fur. *Click!*

"I called the police right away," Mr. Troutman added. "I figured they'd want to know about a bear so they could warn people."

"What time did you hear the drumming noises?" I asked.

"About a half hour ago," he said.

I checked the time. It was almost 6:30 p.m.

WHEN: Heard drumming noises around 6 p.m.

"Thank you, Mr. Troutman," I said.

Mr. Troutman began picking up garbage.

Officer Dee had finished inspecting the scene. He walked over to Izzy and me.

"Hi, Officer Dee," I said.

"Hello, Hilde! Hi, Izzy!" he said.

Izzy smiled. "It looks like there really is a bear on the loose!"

"If you girls are thinking about hunting this bear down for a story, I just want to remind you that bears can be *very* dangerous," he said. "If you see a bear, the best thing to do is to wave your arms to make yourself look bigger, and back away slowly. Please be careful."

He handed me the number of a wildlife officer, just in case we saw anything.

"Thanks!" I said.

"We'll be careful," Izzy added.

Officer Dee walked back toward the police station.

Officer Pam
Wildlife Officer
Selinsgrove
555-555-55

My stomach growled. I checked the time. It was 6:40 p.m. Only an hour and twenty minutes before we had to be home for dinner.

Family dinner was usually at 6 p.m. But tonight, Mom and Dad had pushed it to 8 p.m. since they knew we were busy hunting down a big scoop.

"We should look for more clues," I said. "We need to find this bear."

But Izzy didn't hear me. She was looking toward Pine Street. Her mouth was frozen in the shape of a giant *O*.

I followed her gaze.

It was Donnie and Leon.

"The Mean-agers!" I said. "They're coming our way!"

The Mean-agers are a group of Orange Street teenagers known for their rotten attitudes. Earlier today, my *Orange Street News* investigation had caught Donnie and Leon's friend, Maddy, trying to cheat her way to winning the Bake-Off Bonanza.

"I bet they're angry at us for busting Maddy," said Izzy.

"They're going to be meaner than ever!" I said. "But hey, maybe they have information about the bear."

"Sure," Izzy said, rolling her eyes. "Because the Mean-agers are always *so* helpful."

"Well, we have to face them sometime," I said. "Let's get it over with . . ."

45

4 Rumbling Trucks

Donnie and Leon strutted closer. They glared at us like we were cracks on their phone screens.

Sweat gathered on my palms.

Izzy stepped forward. She tried to sound brave. "If you're angry at us about Maddy getting in trouble, then —"

Donnie interrupted. "Don't pee your pants. We aren't here about Maddy."

"You aren't?" I asked.

"Nope," Leon added. "Maddy did some dumb things. She had it coming."

I let out a deep breath. "Have you guys seen or heard anything about a bear?" I asked.

"A bear?" Donnie said. He laughed. "Has the cute little baby reporter been reading fairy tales?"

Leon stepped forward. "We're just checking out all the cool construction trucks going into the forest," he said.

A construction site in the forest? I wonder what they're building in there . . .

VRRRRRUM! A loud rumbling sound came from deep in the forest. It sounded like a really big truck. I made a note.

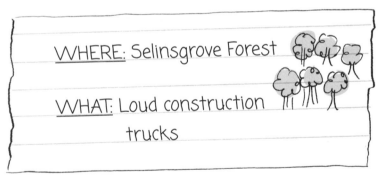

WHERE: Selinsgrove Forest

WHAT: Loud construction
trucks

Donnie and Leon glanced at each other.

"Follow that sound!" yelled Donnie.

The boys disappeared into the forest.

"It's almost 7 p.m.," said Izzy, checking her phone. "Why don't we just head home?"

"Wait!" I said, pointing to a pair of animal tracks in a patch of dry dirt. The tracks were faint, but I could tell they led into the forest.

I started walking toward the trees. Izzy didn't budge.

"Come on, Izzy," I pleaded. "A reporter can't go on an investigation without her photographer! And we *need* to follow these tracks!"

"I don't know, Hilde. Remember Officer Dee's warning: Bears can be very dangerous," she said.

"We don't even know for sure if these are bear tracks," I argued.

Izzy dug her feet into the ground.

I could feel my heart beating in my chest. I knew going after a bear wasn't the best idea, but I *really* wanted to be the one to break this story — even if that meant going in alone.

I took a deep breath and stepped into the forest.

5 Into the Forest

I stood all by myself just inside the forest. I waited, hoping Izzy would follow.

"I'm coming," Izzy said. "But if I see a giant bear, don't expect me to stick around for a picture."

"Deal!" I said, smiling.

We walked deeper into the forest. Tree branches blocked the sunlight, creating long dark shadows all around us. There were tall weeds and prickers everywhere. Izzy and I picked up sticks that were lying nearby. We used them to help create a path.

Izzy shook her head. "Going into the forest when a bear is on the loose? This is crazy, even for you, Hilde," she said.

Leaves crunched under our feet. They sounded like crumpling papers.

"A news reporter has to stay focused on uncovering the truth," I said. "We need to find the bear and figure out why it came into town."

"Yeah, if we don't become bear snacks first!" said Izzy.

VRRRRRUM! The rumbling sound was so loud I covered my ears.

"That must be a giant construction project," said Izzy.

From our spot up on the hill, we could see a clearing below. A large truck hauling long pieces of wood went rambling up a dirt road.

We kept following the animal tracks deeper into the forest. Soon, we reached a dried-up creek bed full of pebbles. The tracks ended at the rocky riverbank.

"The tracks are gone!" I said.

"What now?" asked Izzy.

"Let's just go a bit farther," I said. "If we don't pick up the tracks again, then we'll turn around."

"Good plan," Izzy said, walking along the riverbank. "Hey, look!" She pointed to a patch of mud.

I looked down. Izzy had found the tracks!

She snapped a picture. *Click!*

"That definitely looks like a bear paw," I said, gulping.

Click!

VRRRRRUM! Another truck roared by. The sound made my insides shake.

We kept walking. I followed Izzy, keeping my eyes on the tracks. But then I bumped into her. She had stopped walking.

"Hilde, is your stomach growling?" she whispered.

I listened. But I couldn't hear anything. Then — *GRRRRRRRRR!* The growl was so loud I nearly jumped out of my socks!

"That sounded like . . . a giant bear!" I screamed.

"Hilde, we need to wave our arms and back away slowly — just like Officer Dee told us!" Izzy yelled.

We started walking backward. Izzy tripped over a tangled bush of prickers! Then I tripped over Izzy!

Izzy got back up quickly. I tried to get to my feet, too, but my shirt was tangled in a jagged pricker bush.

Izzy tugged on my shirt. But it was really stuck! We could tell from the sound of crunching leaves that something was coming closer. It was about to be right next to us!

6 A Brown Blur

Izzy was still pulling at my sleeve to untangle it from the pricker bush.

"Hurry!" I screamed.

Just as Izzy got my sleeve free, a blur of fur raced through the trees straight past us.

"Bear!" Izzy cried, pointing.

"Whoa! That was close!" I said. "And you saw the bear?!"

"Yeah," Izzy agreed. "It went running back toward town!"

I brushed off my shirt.

"Did you get a picture?" I asked.

Izzy narrowed her eyes. "I was sort of busy saving your life!"

Izzy was right. "Sorry," I said.

Izzy smiled, but then a serious look came over her face. "Now, we should call that wildlife officer," she said.

That's right. Officer Dee said we were supposed to call Officer Pam if we saw the bear. But could we be sure what we *really* saw?

"Are you positive you saw a bear?" I asked.

Izzy shook her head slowly. "No," she said. "But it was furry and big and fast."

"There *are* lots of deer in the forest," I pointed out. "Are you sure it wasn't a deer?"

"Well, I guess I can't really be sure," Izzy said, rubbing her chin.

"Then maybe it's best not to call until we have more facts," I said. "Especially considering Officer Dee warned us about chasing after bears."

Izzy nodded. "I guess with all the construction noise, I'm not even sure we heard a growl . . ."

"See? We need proof before we call for back-up," I said. "How much time do we have before dinner?"

Izzy looked at her phone. "Thirty minutes," she said.

We quickly traced our path back through the forest. By the time we made it back to Grove Grocer, it was getting dark.

We hopped on Izzy's bike. She pedaled up Pine Street and turned right on Orange.

Then we heard yelling. It was coming from Rotary Park.

"It sounds like someone's in trouble over at the park!" said Izzy.

"Let's go investigate!" I said.

"Okay," she said. "Hang on!"

Izzy cut a hard right. We jumped the curb and took a shortcut to Rotary Park. Seconds later, Izzy skidded to a stop at the park gate.

The yelling was coming from inside the playhouse castle. Joey and Kristen — two first graders who lived across the street from our house — jumped up and ran over as soon as they saw us. They looked like they had seen a ghost!

"You aren't going to believe what just happened!" Joey shouted.

7 Bear!

"Can you tell us what happened?" I asked Joey and Kristen.

"There was a giant bear in the park!" said Kristen. "It almost ate us!"

Witnesses! I needed to know exactly what they saw and where they saw it.

"Start at the beginning," I said.

Joey pointed to the playhouse castle. "We were inside there. We were trying to see who could hit the center circle of the merry-go-round first with rocks. That's when we heard a scary growling noise."

"It was a giant bear with huge teeth!" Kristen added.

"Yeah," said Joey. "It had huge claws and it was making this sound like *grrrooowll!*"

Izzy turned to me. "That sounds like the same growl we heard in Selinsgrove Forest."

"That means we really did hear a bear! It must've run this way!" I said. I wrote everything down, then turned to Izzy. "If the bear was just here, where is it now?"

"I'm not sure," Izzy replied. "But it's definitely time to call Officer Pam."

I kept interviewing Joey and Kristen, while Izzy called Officer Pam to tell her what happened.

"What did the bear look like exactly?" I asked.

"W-w-well," Joey sputtered. He scratched the side of his head. Then he looked at Kristen.

Kristen looked at the ground. "We're not sure what it looked like," she said.

"What do you mean?" I asked.

"Well, as soon as we heard the growl, we ducked down and hid," said Joey.

I stopped writing. "If you didn't see it, then how do you two know it was a *giant* bear with *huge* claws and teeth?" I asked.

"We heard the scariest growl ever," said Joey. "Don't you believe us?"

"It's not about believing or not believing, Joey," I said. "I report facts. The fact is that you heard a growling noise. But it is also a fact that you did not *see* a bear."

WHERE: Rotary Park

GROWL
GROWL

WHAT: growling sounds

GROWL
GROWL

Suddenly, I heard Izzy call out, "Over here!"
She was taking pictures of the sandbox.

There were large animal tracks in the sand.
They were pointing in the direction of Orange
Street. These tracks were even clearer than the
ones in the forest. Each paw print had five little
toe marks!

Click!

"More tracks! Good work, Izzy!" I said. "So what did Officer Pam say?"

"She said she'd investigate the area," Izzy replied, "and that we should all head home."

"We told you there was a bear!" said Kristen.

"Time for bed!" Joey and Kristen's mom called out.

I looked at the time. "It's 7:50," I said.

"We've got to go, too!" said Izzy.

Just then, we heard sirens.

"I know that sound!" I said. "That's the sound of breaking news!"

Izzy and I jumped on her bike. We cut back through a neighbor's yard and saw flashing lights. It looked like they were right outside our house!

8 Pool Party

As Izzy pedaled closer, we could see that a police car wasn't parked in front of our house. It was at our next-door neighbor Sue's house.

Izzy leaned her bike against the telephone pole. She got her camera ready.

"I hope the bear didn't hurt Brian!" I said. Brian is Sue's adorable pet pig.

We ran over to the fence that separated our backyard from Sue's. We could hear someone talking. We cupped our ears to the wood to try to listen. A good reporter knows when to snoop!

But we still couldn't hear what they were saying!

We waited.

Finally, the gate opened and Officer Wentworth walked out. He's always so grumpy looking! As he drove away, we called to Sue over the fence. She waved us over. We ran into her backyard.

I pulled out my notepad.

"Hi," Sue said. "Are you girls here as nosy neighbors or as reporters?"

"Both!" I said, smiling. "Is everything okay? Can you tell us why Officer Wentworth was here?"

"Have a look," she said. Sue had a large swimming pool. She pointed at the pool gate behind us.

We walked over to investigate.

Brian ran out into the yard. Sue laughed. Brian was squealing. It sounded like someone let the air out of a helium balloon. He came over to us. Izzy and I pet his smooth, pink back.

But I knew we had to hurry. I turned back to the gate.

"Whoa," I said.

The latch that kept the gate door locked was broken! There were scratch marks near it. Izzy took a picture.

Click!

"That's not all," said Sue. "Brian's food dish was broken — and it was empty. All of his dried fruits were gone!"

I wrote everything down.

WHERE: Sue's pool

WHAT: scratch marks and a broken lock
on the gate to Sue's pool, and
Brian's food is missing

"Is there anything else?" I asked.

Sue scratched her head. "Not really, but Officer Wentworth did say he's worried a bear might be on the loose. So I'm keeping Brian inside tonight."

"That's a good idea," I said.

"He also gave me the number of Officer Pam. He said to call her if I see the bear," she added. "Be careful, girls."

"We will," I said. "Thank you."

As we walked back to our yard, Izzy pulled up the picture of the bird feeder. "Look!" she said. "These scratches look the same as the ones on Sue's pool gate!"

"You're right!" I agreed. "The animal that took down that bird feeder is the same one that attacked that gate!"

Izzy looked at the time. It was 7:59!

"Hilde!" Izzy cried. "If we don't get home in one minute, Dad's growl will be scarier than that giant bear!"

9 Enchilada Time!

Izzy and I rushed inside.

"We're home!" we called out.

"Just in time," Mom said as she set a warm plate of enchiladas down on the table. Steam rose off the bubbly, cheesy top. I couldn't wait to dig in!

My little sisters Georgie's and Juliet's chairs were empty. They were already in bed.

"What big scoop are my daughters on now?" Dad asked. He took a spoonful of black beans.

"We're working on a huge story!" Izzy said.

"And we almost got eaten by a giant bear!" I added.

"A giant bear?" Dad said. He raised his eyebrows like he does when he thinks we are pranking him.

Then Mom sat down. That meant we could start eating.

"Well, why don't you invite your furry friend for dinner?" she said. "We have enough enchiladas to share."

Mom and Dad both laughed.

Izzy rolled her eyes.

"They'll believe us when they read our story," I whispered to her.

Izzy nodded. "Yeah, but we need to get back to work!"

I quickly shoveled food into my mouth until my plate was clean. Izzy did, too.

"Hungry?" Mom said, smiling. "That's good because there's a warm cobbler for dessert. I made it with fresh berries from our wild blueberry bush out back."

We finished dessert faster than dinner!

We cleaned up the dinner dishes, then ran upstairs to my room.

Izzy and I sat down on the floor.

"Time to review our notes," I said as I opened my notepad.

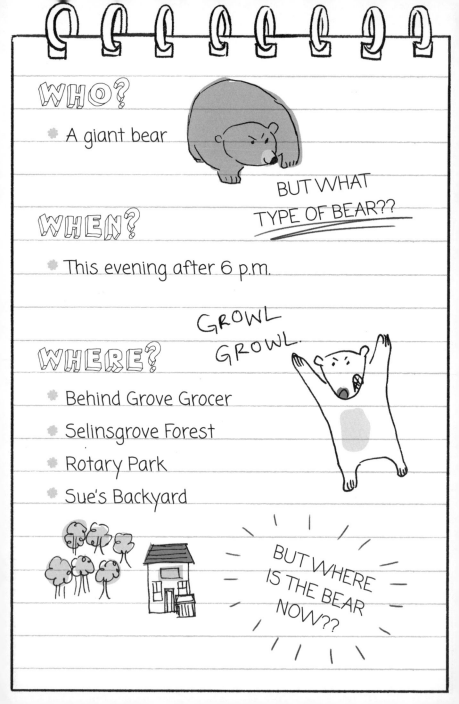

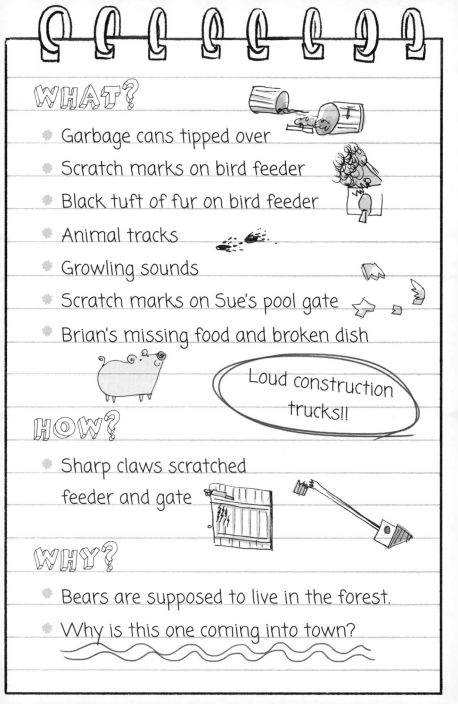

WHAT?

* Garbage cans tipped over
* Scratch marks on bird feeder
* Black tuft of fur on bird feeder
* Animal tracks
* Growling sounds
* Scratch marks on Sue's pool gate
* Brian's missing food and broken dish

Loud construction trucks!!

HOW?

* Sharp claws scratched feeder and gate

WHY?

* Bears are supposed to live in the forest.
* Why is this one coming into town?

I put down my notepad.

"We need to figure out why this bear is in town," I said, "and where it might head next."

"Let's do some research," Izzy said.

She began looking up information about bears.

"The most common type of bear found in Pennsylvania is the black bear," she said.

"Wait," I said. "The fur Mr. Troutman found was black!"

"Great! So it is probably a black bear. Let me see if I can find out what black bears like to do and eat," she said.

Izzy typed some more.

"Black bears love to swim. They eat wild berries — and also trash," she read aloud.

"What else does it say?" I asked.

"Hmmmmm," she said. "Black bears are increasingly being pushed out of their homes by new development."

"New development?" I asked.

"That means construction — like those trucks we saw in Selinsgrove Forest," Izzy explained.

Izzy turned toward me. I couldn't help but laugh. The corners of her mouth were stained blue from the blueberry cobbler. She wiped her mouth.

Then it hit me!

"Izzy, I know how we're going to crack this case wide open," I said.

10 Campout

I jumped up. "Listen, Izzy: Bears love berries!"

"Yeah, so? I told you that," Izzy responded. "What's your bright idea?"

"Well, we know the bear is close by. And we have a berry bush! So we can pick berries," I said, sketching my ideas on paper. "We can make a trail of berries from Sue's pool gate — where it was last seen — to our berry bush. Hopefully, the bear will follow the trail right into our backyard! Then we can call Officer Pam to come get it!"

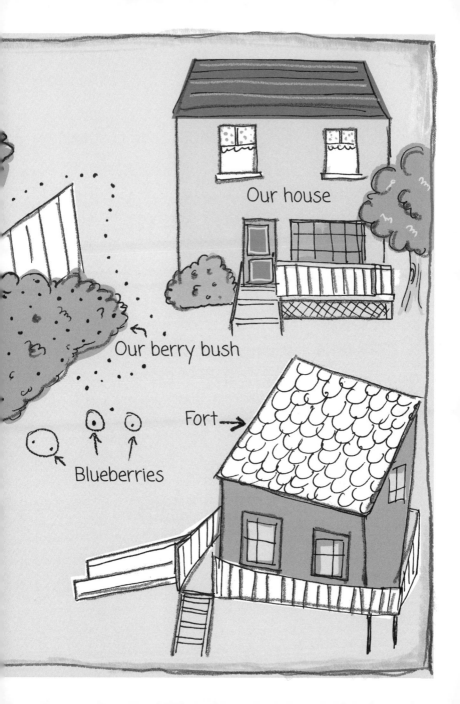

Izzy's eyes grew wide. "If the bear comes into our yard, then we can take the picture we need for our article!"

"Exactly!" I said. "We should camp out in the Fort tonight."

We called it the Fort, but it was actually a wooden playhouse with a long plastic slide. It had a little room on top with a window and a door that latched.

"Sleeping outside with a bear on the loose sounds risky," Izzy said.

"There is a strong metal latch on the Fort door," I said. "We'll be safe in there."

Izzy thought it over. "Okay," she said. "Let's do this!"

First, we picked berries off the bush in our backyard. Next, we made the berry trail. Finally, we placed a small pile of berries outside Sue's pool gate.

"Perfect!" I said. "Now you get our pillows. I'll let Mom and Dad know we'll be sleeping outside. And I'll grab snacks!"

"Hey, why do you get to grab the snacks?" Izzy asked, scrunching up her nose.

"The reporter always handles the snacks," I said.

Izzy laughed. "I know you just made that up, but whatever. See you in the Fort!"

I let Mom and Dad know where we'd be. Then I grabbed a plate of brownies.

When I got to the Fort, Izzy was near the window, checking her camera.

"Remember," I said. "A great picture can turn a *good* story into an *amazing* story!"

Izzy smiled as she propped her camera up on a tripod. Then she spotted the brownies.

"Score!" she said, biting into one.

We leaned back against the wall of the Fort.

"I'll take first lookout," Izzy offered.

"Okay," I said. "I'll start to work on my article."

I took out my phone and began to type . . . But soon, my eyelids began to feel heavy. I couldn't help it. It had been such a crazy, long day. I drifted to sleep.

SPLASH! A loud noise woke me up. A soft pinkish-orange light was coming through the Fort window. It was early morning. I rubbed my eyes.

I looked over at Izzy. Her eyes were closed.

"Wake up, Izzy!" I yelled.

She sprung up like a jack-in-the-box.

"Did you hear that?" I asked.

"Hear what?" she said.

SPLASH! I heard it again. It was coming from Sue's pool!

11 Investigate!

Izzy pointed her camera at the pool. *Click!*

"What is it?" I asked. "What do you see?"

"I can't get a good look," she said. "There's definitely *something* in the pool. We're just too far away."

I looked through my notes. Bears love to swim!

"Izzy!" I said. "I bet it's the bear! Zoom in!"

Izzy adjusted her camera lens. "I'm trying," she said.

I grabbed my notepad and unlatched the Fort door.

"Hilde!" Izzy cried. "Where are you going?"

"I need to investigate!" I said.

"Are you crazy?!" Izzy yelled. She grabbed my arm.

I wiggled free. "I'm just going to take a quick peek over the fence. I'll be right back," I said.

"No way!" shouted Izzy. "We need to stay safely behind this door!"

I turned, burst out the door, and slid down the slide.

I sprinted to the fence.

I pulled myself up with my arms to peek my head over. But I couldn't hold myself up well enough to see over the top. My feet landed on the ground with a thud. And my notepad fell out of my pocket.

I reached down to pick it up. That's when I realized that someone — or *something* — was right behind me!

I was about to scream when I heard a familiar voice.

"Here," Izzy said. She handed me my notepad. I took it from her.

"I thought you were staying in the Fort?" I whispered.

"Who is going to save my little sister from a giant bear if I'm not around?" she said.

"Thanks," I said. "Now let's get a look over this fence!"

Izzy hoisted me up on her shoulders. The first thing I noticed was that Sue's pool gate was open again. Next, I saw wet paw prints leading away from the pool.

Then I saw something move. I looked over at a large bush in Sue's yard.

I froze.

Two round, black eyes were looking back at me.

13 B-B-Bear!

I stared over the fence into Sue's yard.

"Izzy," I sputtered. "It's the b-b-bear!"

"Quick!" Izzy yelled. "Call Officer Pam!"

I reached into my pocket to grab my phone, but my hands were shaking. I dropped it — into Sue's yard!

"Hilde!" screamed Izzy.

The sound of the phone hitting the ground startled the bear. It darted out! I gasped. At first, I thought my eyes were playing tricks on me . . .

It *was* a bear! But it wasn't a *giant* bear. It was just about the cutest thing I had ever seen! It had black fur and wasn't much bigger than a fire hydrant.

The bear cub wasn't going to eat us! But it was clearly hungry. It spotted our berry pile near the gate. Then it started following the trail of wild berries.

"Izzy, the bear's just a baby!" I said. "And it's headed for our yard!"

Izzy pulled me down from her shoulders. We ran up onto our back porch.

Just then, Dad came outside.

"I heard screaming! Is everyone o—?" he asked, following our gaze to the bear.

"Whoa!" Dad exclaimed.

"We told you there was a bear on the loose," Izzy said.

"That's true," Dad said. "I should've listened to you girls!"

"You looked scared, Dad," I said, laughing. "It's just a cute little baby bear!"

"That cub might look cute," Dad said, "but the mama bear is probably close behind. Mama bears can be very dangerous when they think a baby is in danger."

Izzy took pictures of the bear. *Click! Click!*

I borrowed Dad's phone and called Officer Pam.

"We found the bear. It's in our yard right now!" I said.

I gave her my address.

"I will be right there! Thank you, Hilde!" she said.

Mom opened the door. "Get inside right now — all three of you!" she said.

Mom and Dad scooted us into the house. We watched from the kitchen window.

The bear couldn't eat enough berries!

"I wonder how this little cub got all the way here," Dad said.

"I can answer that," I said, smiling. "Loud construction noises scared the bear out of the forest. That's why he left. Then he got hungry and went looking for food. First, he found Mr. Troutman's garbage."

My dad nodded.

"Next, the bear ran through Rotary Park. That's probably when he smelled Brian's dried fruits," I continued. "That's why he scratched the fence to Sue's pool gate — to get to the food. After a bit of exploring, the bear came back and went for a swim just because bears like swimming. But the bear got hungry again."

"That's when he found our berry trail, leading him right to our berry bush," added Izzy.

"I don't know how I feel about my daughters leading bears to our house," Mom said.

"Don't worry, Mom. We called Officer Pam," I said. "She's on her way."

Just then, we heard a knock on the door.

14 Back in the Wild

I ran to answer the door. A woman in a brown uniform stood on our doorstep. She had a golden star-shaped badge pinned to her shirt.

"Hi, I'm Pam, the wildlife officer," she said.

"Hi, I'm Hilde — the reporter for the *Orange Street News*," I said.

"Nice to meet you," Pam said. "Now where's this bear you found?"

I led Officer Pam to the window.

"You did the right thing by calling right away. If it wasn't for your hard work, there could have been real problems for the residents of Selinsgrove — and for this young cub," Officer Pam said. "Now please wait here while I safely catch the cub."

Officer Pam went to her van and pulled out a large wire cage. She placed the cage in the middle of our yard. Then she threw food pellets near and inside the cage and slowly backed away. She had made a trail just like ours!

We waited, quietly watching from the window.

The cub finished eating blueberries. He put his little nose in the air, and wandered over to the pellets inside the cage.

Suddenly, the cage door shut.

The little cub really didn't seem to notice he was trapped. He just kept eating.

Officer Pam carried the cage to her van. All four of us ran outside. I dashed next door and picked up my phone. Then I ran back.

Officer Pam turned to me and Izzy. "This black bear cub didn't want to hurt or scare anyone. He probably just got scared by the construction going on in Selinsgrove Forest and wandered into town looking for food," she explained.

That was a great quote for my article! I wrote it down word for word.

"That's just what Hilde said!" Dad exclaimed. I could tell he was proud of me.

"Where will you take the cub?" I asked.

"Back to the forest," replied Officer Pam. "I need to try to reunite him with his mama."

"Can we come?" asked Izzy.

Officer Pam smiled. "You two are the reason we found this bear today. So, of course you can come! That is, so long as it's all right with your parents."

"I think that's a bear-y good idea!" Dad said.

Izzy and I jumped up and down.

Wildlife Pa

15 Mama Bear

Izzy and I saw the bear cub behind us. He was sleeping! His little paws were snuggled against his tiny face.

"He's so cute!" I whispered. "I just want to eat him!"

"You want to eat everything," Izzy joked.

Officer Pam drove down a bumpy road into Selinsgrove Forest. After several minutes, she stopped the van.

"I can tell from the scratches on these trees that this is where a family of bears lives," Officer Pam said, pointing at the marked trees. "So this cub's mama might be close by. You two wait here."

Izzy and I pressed up to the window as Officer Pam walked around back. She gently set the cage on the ground and slowly opened it.

The cub was still sleeping. Officer Pam hurried back and drove the van a short distance down the hill.

"There," she said, parking the van. "Now we wait."

We waited.

Finally, a large, black bear came lumbering down the hill.

"That bear is huge!" said Izzy.

"She must be the mama!" I said.

"That's right," Officer Pam said.

Izzy zoomed in and began taking pictures.
Click! Click!

The mama bear went up to her cub. She nudged him playfully. The cub woke up and nuzzled his mama's nose.

"He looks so happy!" Izzy said.

"He is," Officer Pam answered. She smiled.

The bears ran up the hill, and disappeared behind the tree line.

VRRRRRUM! A construction truck rumbled by.

I frowned. "Those trucks are so loud. How do we know the bear cub won't get scared again and head back into town?"

"We don't," replied Officer Pam. "We just have to hope that the forest animals can adjust to all the changes. And hopefully, the bear cub will stay closer to his mama now. But don't worry, girls. Officers like me will always be here to help them out."

As Officer Pam drove us home, I finished typing my story. Izzy chose great photos, too. I posted the article online by 8 a.m.!

When we got out of the van, Officer Pam handed Izzy and me two golden, star-shaped badges — just like the one she was wearing.

"Now you're honorary wildlife officers," she said. "No one knew where that baby cub was until you two cracked the case!"

We pinned the badges to our shirts.

"Wow!" I said. "Thanks!"

"This is awesome," added Izzy.

Just then, we heard sirens.

"That sounds like a fire truck!" I said.

Izzy looked at me.

"Hilde, are you thinking what I'm thinking?" she asked.

"Let's follow those sirens, Izzy!" I shouted. "This next adventure is going to be HOT!"

"This black bear cub didn't want to hurt or scare anyone. He probably just got scared by the construction going on in Selinsgrove Forest and wandered into town looking for food," Officer Pam told the *Orange Street News.* [4]

"It is a good thing we found this bear, because even a young cub can cause a lot of damage, or even hurt itself," Officer Pam added. [5]

The cub was reunited with its mama this morning in Selinsgrove Forest. [6]

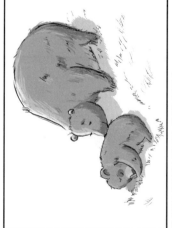

PHOTO CREDIT: ISABEL ROSE LYSIAK

1. HEADLINE 2. LEDE 3. NUT 4. QUOTE 5. SUPPORT 6. KICKER

WHO? Hilde Lysiak

WHAT? Hilde is the real-life publisher of her own newspaper, the *Orange Street News*! You can read her work at www.orangestreetnews.com.

WHEN? Hilde began her newspaper when she was seven years old with crayons and paper. Today, she has millions of readers!

WHERE? Hilde lives in Selinsgrove, Pennsylvania.

WHY? Hilde loves adventure, is super curious, and believes that you don't have to be a grown-up to do great things in the world!

HOW? Tips from people just like you make Hilde's newspaper possible!

Matthew Lysiak is Hilde's dad and coauthor. He is a former reporter for the *New York Daily News*.

Joanne Lew-Vriethoff was born in Malaysia and grew up in Los Angeles. She received her B.A. in illustration from Art Center College of Design in Pasadena. Today, Joanne lives in Amsterdam, where she spends much of her time illustrating children's books.